КАТ Я

Katya of Fort Ross

KATYA

of

FORT ROSS

by
Clara Stites
illustrated by Cindy Davis

2001 · Fithian Press, Santa Barbara, California

Published by Fithian Press
A division of Daniel and Daniel, Publishers, Inc.
Post Office Box 1525
Santa Barbara, CA 93102
www.danielpublishing.com

LIBRARY OF CONGRESS CATALOGING-IN-PUBLICATION DATA
Stites, Clara, (date)
  Katya of Fort Ross / by Clara Stites.
      p.   cm.
  Summary: In the mid-nineteenth century Katya, a Russian girl
whose stepmother is Aleut, and Miyacha, a native Kashaya girl,
trade knowledge about their cultures as they play together in and
near Fort Ross, a Russian settlement in northern California.
Includes historical information about the fort.
  ISBN 1-56474-379-9 (pbk. : alk. paper)
  1. Fort Ross (Calif.)—History—Juvenile fiction. [1. Fort Ross
(Calif.)—History—Fiction. 2. Russians—California—Fiction. 3.
Kashaya Indians—Fiction. 4. Aleuts—Fiction. 5. Indians of North
America—California—Fiction. 6. California—History—To 1846—
Fiction.]   I. Title.
PZ7.S8613 Kat 2001
[Fic]—dc21
                        00-012691

For Ms. Dwyer's fourth-grade class,
Strawberry School,
Bennett Valley School District,
Santa Rosa, California

Special thanks to the knowledgeable and helpful people at Fort Ross State Historic Park, especially Jeff Meierhenry, Lake Perry, and Bill Walton, and to Katia Jacobs for sharing her name.

Katya's Family and Friends

Katya, a ten-year-old Russian girl who lives on the California coast with her father and her stepmother. Her name is a nickname for *Ekaterina* in Russian. Other nicknames that her family and friends might call her are *Katiusha* and *Katinka*.

Petr Aleksei, Katya's father, who works as the master carpenter at Fort Ross, the southernmost Russian settlement in North America.

Tatuin Marie, a wise native Alaskan woman who is married to Katya's father and understands Katya and her secrets.

Miyacha, a lively Kashaya girl who becomes friends with Katya and shares many new experiences with her.

Miyacha's mother, who shows Katya how to make acorn soup.

Miyacha's grandmother, who weaves stories into her baskets.

КАТЯ

Katya of Fort Ross

Chapter 1

Katya's Secret

Katya knew the shady places where the wild primroses blossomed and the rocky crevices where the sea birds laid their fragile eggs. She had seen the whales swim past, and she had discovered the home of the sea otter and her pup.

The sun on Katya's face was warm, and the sound of the waves was like gentle music. She sat absolutely still and watched the water. The otters were always hard to see because they floated among the strange pods of kelp. The ocean moved forward and back, the kelp

moved with the waves, gulls swooped over-
head. Katya waited.

Years ago, she knew, there had been thou-
sands of sea otters along the California coast.
She had heard her father and the Aleut hunters talking of the old days, the days when the
sea otters were so trusting and easy to catch.
But those days were gone; hunters had killed
most of the sea otters. She had been lucky to
find this mother and her pup. She had told
no one about them, not even her father.

Then Katya saw them! The mother sea otter drifted peacefully near the foot of the cliff.
She held her sleeping baby on her chest and
looked at Katya with bright, inquisitive eyes.
Katya had watched the otter teach her pup to
dive and use a stone to break open the spiny
shells of sea urchins. She loved the way the
otters swam and dove and played. Best of all,
she loved the way the mother and her baby
held hands as they slept in the kelp. That
way, they would not drift apart.

14

Katya thought of her own mother, who had died six years before. If Katya had held tight to her mother's hand, would they still be together? But she knew her mother was buried in the cold ground of Sitka, Alaska, while she and her father and her stepmother, Tatuin Marie, were here in California.

Tatuin Marie was an Eskimo woman with heavy, dark hair. Katya's hair curled in exuberant ringlets and was golden-red like her mother's. Sometimes she wished it were straight and dark like the hair of Tatuin Marie or the Kashaya children at Fort Ross. Then she would think of her red-haired mother, and be glad that she looked like her.

It was time to return to the village. Katya waved goodbye to the otters and climbed to the top of the cliff. When she looked back, all she could see was kelp.

As she walked across the open meadow, she could pick out the gray roofs of Fort Ross. The late afternoon sun lit up the gabled roof of the big house where the commandant lived and the two towers of the church with their Russian crosses. Katya could hear the bells ringing the hour and the shouts of the children who lived in the houses outside the fort. Her house was there too, and her old brown pony stood near the door. She stopped to stroke his neck. "When no one is watching, I will bring you sugar," she whispered into his furry ear. He snorted softly and pushed his nose against her shoulder.

When she went inside the house, Tatuin Marie had a piece of fresh-baked bread and a cup of tea ready. Katya liked Tatuin Marie. She leaned against her stepmother's chair and let the tea warm her inside and out.

"Wandering again, eh?" Tatuin Marie asked.

Katya nodded.

"And where do you go on these long afternoons? You are a girl of many secrets, but I think they are good secrets."

16

Katya finished her bread, and Tatuin Marie gave her a second piece. "When you have finished eating, your father has something to show you. Perhaps you should go to where he is working."

Katya's father was Petr Aleksei, master carpenter for Fort Ross. Others before him had built the first buildings and the high walls, but Petr Aleksei had made most of the furniture for the barracks, the store, and the houses of the officers and commandant. He knew how to shape the wood of the redwood and the oak. He could repair the carved driftwood frames of the *baidarkas* or cut decorative designs into cupboards or tables. He carved canes for the old people and small wooden bears or birds for the children.

When Katya found him that afternoon, he was rubbing oil into the richly grained wood of a bowl. "Katya," he said, "look. Do you think that Tatuin Marie will like this bowl I have made for her? It is applewood."

Katya touched the bowl with her fingertips. The wood felt smooth, like satin. "It is beautiful, Papa Petr," she said. Was this what he had wanted her to see? A bowl for Tatuin Marie?

"And for you, my dearest Katinka, I have this," he said. He pulled a soft piece of cloth off of a small wooden chest. Katya saw that the chest was painted with a bright design of birds and flowers. It had an iron lock set into its front, and the name *Katya* just above the lock. "For all your treasures," her father said. "Do you like it?"

"Oh, Papa. Is it truly mine?"

"Yes. Yours and only yours. Shall I carry it to the house for you?"

Katya ran beside him through the dusk of evening. The moon was rising over the fort, and she could hear piano music from the commandant's house. She thought that she had never been so happy.

Chapter 2
Miyacha

In the morning, Katya carried the box Papa Petr had made outside into the sunlight. Its bright painted birds and flowers looked almost alive in the morning light. Carefully she turned the key and opened the lid. The inside of the box was unpainted wood, and into it Papa Petr had built small, rectangular compartments.

Tatuin Marie came from where she was working in their family's fenced garden. "You like your Papa Petr's box, I can see," she said.

"Yes," said Katya. "And here is my first treasure." She held up the little sea otter that Tatuin Marie had given her a year before. The otter was carved from white bone. It lay on its back, hands on its chest, feet pointing to the sky. Katya lined one of the compartments with soft grass and laid the carved otter gently into it. "But for today I will leave the lid open so that my otter can see the sun," she told Tatuin Marie.

"Ah, good. Now that the otter is safe, perhaps you will find time to help me in the garden," said Tatuin Marie, so Katya went with her to plant the new potatoes.

Later that day, Katya went back to the cliff to watch for her real, live otters. The sea was rough, and she could not see the otters. She waited for a long time. While she waited, she gathered the bird feathers that had blown and caught in the low bushes. She would carry the feathers home and put them into her box of secret treasures.

Finally, she grew tired of waiting for the otters. She tucked the feathers safely into the waist of her skirt and climbed down closer to the sea. Soon she was on the beach. The dark sand was covered with driftwood and kelp and huge rocks that had tumbled from the cliffs above.

She walked toward the edge of the water, hoping to see the otters. Then a wave bigger than the others surprised her, surging cold, foamy water up around her legs. Katya jumped back, but she slipped in the sand and fell. The next wave crashed over her head and pushed her along the beach. Katya knew the danger of the waves. Frightened, she scrambled quickly to safety before the next wave could reach her. She was wet all over, but she was safe.

Katya stood up and tried to shake the wet sand off of her clothes and out of her hair. Suddenly she heard a sound behind her. It sounded like laughter, but perhaps it was just the cry of a gull. Then she heard a voice, and she turned.

Not five feet away from Katya stood a Kashaya girl. Her face was wide and smiling, and her eyes were very dark. Katya had never seen this girl before; she was not one of the girls from the Kashaya village beside Fort Ross, nor was she one of the Creole children of mixed parentage. Why was she here, alone on the beach? Had she been watching Katya all this time?

Katya could speak a little of the Kashaya dialect. "Are you lost?" she asked the girl.

The girl laughed again and pressed her hands together. She shook her head "no" and then repeated Katya's question. "Are *you* lost?"

"No," said Katya, "but I am very wet."

"You are Very Wet. I am Miyacha," said the girl.

"You are Miyacha. I am Katya. As you see, I am wet, but that is not my name," said Katya.

24

With both hands, she twisted water from her skirt. Miyacha smiled and beckoned with her hand for Katya to follow her.

Between two of the big rocks on the beach, Katya saw an old red blanket spread on the sand. On it were six lengths of kelp with their bulbous heads. "The sun dries them," Miyacha explained. "Sit, and the sun will dry you also."

Katya sat on one corner of the blanket. She realized then that she was shivering. Was it from fear or cold? She did not know. But the sun felt warm and good, and she was glad that she was not alone.

She watched while Miyacha used a sharp stone to cut the long tails off the kelp. She measured each one against her arm before she cut, so that they were all the same length—each a little shorter than her forearm. Then she arranged them carefully again in the sun.

"What are you doing?" Katya asked.

Miyacha picked up one of the pieces of kelp and held it in her arms like a baby. She rocked it gently and made a soft humming sound.

"You are making dolls!" Katya exclaimed.

Miyacha nodded. She touched her own eyes, then she touched the head of the kelp doll. She touched her mouth and nose, then the head of kelp. She lifted the edge of the red blanket and wrapped it around the kelp. "When they are ready," Miyacha said, "I will give them eyes to see and mouths to talk and blankets to warm them."

Katya remembered the feathers she had gathered on the cliff top. They were still safe inside the waist of her skirt, though they were wet and not so pretty as before. She held them toward Miyacha. "When they are dry, they will be beautiful again," she said. "You can use them to dress your dolls."

"Thank you," Miyacha said. She took the feathers out of Katya's hand and smoothed

26

them flat on the blanket so that their bright colors showed. "I will make a doll for you and name her *Katya!*"

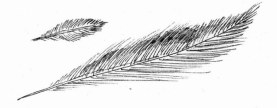

Chapter 3
"Tcim, Tcim, Tcim"

During the summer, Katya never knew when she might see Miyacha. Sometimes weeks would pass without any sign of the lively Kashaya girl. At other times, Miyacha would seem to be everywhere—at the shore, on the path through the meadow, once even high in a tree at the Russian orchard.

Tatuin Marie went often to the orchard. Katya liked to go with her. Together they would look at the blossoms on each tree and predict how much fruit would come at harvest time. When the blossoms were thick,

Tatuin Marie would tell the story she told every year. "When the trees bear well, we must thank the old Russian priest. It was he who sprinkled each tree with holy water when he planted this orchard."

On warm days, Tatuin Marie and Katya would sit down in the shade of an apple tree and watch the patterns that waves, wind, and sun made on the ocean far below. Sometimes they would see hawks gliding over the meadows, or Katya would lie on her back in the grass and make up stories about the clouds.

That is what she was doing the day that Miyacha met Tatuin Marie. Katya had pointed to a long, dark cloud. "The dark boat is carrying the Aleut hunters across the sky," she told her stepmother. "The brave hunters will search the clouds, but they will not find a single sea otter."

Just as Katya finished speaking, she heard the clapping of hands above her. Jumping to her feet, she peered up into the leafy branches. First she saw only a slim brown foot. Then Miyacha sprang down from the tree, laughing as she always did.

Katya had not told anyone about her new friend. Quickly, she motioned with her hand for Miyacha to go away. But, of course, Tatuin Marie had heard the rustle of leaves and the girl's bright laughter. She came to stand beside Katya. "Is this one of your secrets, Katya?" she asked. "If so, it is one you must share with your father and me. "

Miyacha walked back with them to Katya's little house outside the fort. Katya could see her looking at the high gate to the fort. "You are safe," she reassured her. "The walls are only for show, and the cannon have never been fired at an enemy."

Tatuin Marie made three cups of tea in the blue-and-white cups. Miyacha laughed out loud when Tatuin Marie handed her the cup. She held the cup up in the air and looked at

31

its bottom. Then she set it on the table and turned it slowly so that she could see the little people and birds painted on it. Finally, she lifted the cup in both hands and sipped from it and laughed again.

"Why do you laugh?" asked Katya.

Miyacha moved the cup toward Katya. "We have nothing like this. What is it made of?" she asked.

Katya had never thought about the cup at all. Her family had plates and cups. She used them every day. But where had they come from? She looked over at Tatuin Marie.

"They are cups from a country we call China," Tatuin Marie said. "The Russians and the Chinese have been trading things back and forth for many, many years. Papa Petr and I brought the cups when we came here on the boat from Sitka. Before that, I think, those cups belonged to your mother, Katya."

Now Katya held her own cup in the air and looked at its bottom. There were words there and tiny numbers, but she could not read them. Then she put the cup down and looked carefully at its decorations. There was a woman on a bridge, there a tree with long weeping branches, there a bird flying above the bridge. Now it was Katya's turn to laugh. "I never noticed them before," she said.

Tatuin Marie nodded. "Yes, you are so busy looking at the clouds and the waves that you do not see what is right before you."

When she finished her tea, Katya left the table and returned with the box her father had made. She set it in front of Miyacha and motioned for her to open it. Miyacha ran her hands over the box, tracing the flowers and the letters of Katya's name. Then she opened the cover and lifted out the carved otter. Smiling, she cradled it in her hand and made the motions of the waves. Katya wondered if Miyacha knew about the sea otter and her pup.

"Come, shall we go outside?" she asked.

Miyacha followed her, and they walked through the big gate of the fort and across the yard to where Papa Petr had his carpenter's shop. He was inside, peeling long golden curls of wood off of an axe handle that he was making.

Katya was almost afraid to let her father meet Miyacha. What if he forbade her to see this little girl because she was not Russian?

But she need not have worried, because Papa Petr put down the axe handle and smiled at both girls. "Come in," he said. "I am happy to meet a friend of my daughter's."

Miyacha was very quiet, looking down at her feet. Katya tried to imagine Papa Petr through the other girl's eyes. He was so tall, and his hair and his beard were curly and brown. He wore heavy boots and woolen pants and a loose shirt of rough heavy cotton that Tatuin Marie had made.

"Sit down, Papa. You are too tall, I think," Katya said.

"Tcim, Tcim, Tcim"

Papa sat on the low stool in front of his tool bench. Now he and Miyacha were the same height. Papa Petr reached behind him and picked up one of the little bears that he carved from redwood. He handed it to Miyacha. "A Russian bear to welcome you," he said. Now, at last, Miyacha laughed her bright laugh. Papa Petr and Katya laughed too.

All the way to the shore, Miyacha held her wooden bear in front of her. "What are you doing?" Katya asked.

"I must show him the world," Miyacha answered.

When they reached the cliff top, Katya could not see the otters, but she and Miyacha sat and watched the water.

Miyacha taught Katya how to play a Kashaya game. They lay on their stomachs, and Miyacha used a bit of wood to make a row of small holes in the ground. With each hole, she said, *"Tcim, tcim, tcim."* The line of little holes grew long in front of Miyacha until finally she was out of breath and had to stop and take air into her lungs.

"Now you," she said. Katya took the stick and pulled a big breath of air into her lungs. Then she began to make a new line of holes next to the ones Miyacha had made. *"Tcim, tcim, tcim,"* she said, but before she was able to make many holes, she needed to take another breath.

Miyacha clapped her hands in happiness. "Try again. You will become better at this game if you practice." With her hand she brushed dirt over the holes Katya had made. Katya took a big breath and began again, *"Tcim, tcim...."* But suddenly Miyacha stopped her and pointed silently at the ocean.

There, in the water at the foot of the cliff, was the mother sea otter. She and her pup looked up toward the girls and seemed to be laughing with them.

Chapter 4

A Basket of Soup

In the autumn, the days grew shorter, and the fog rolled in from the sea and made Katya feel damp all over. Her hair curled more than ever in the wet air. The sea otter and her pup were gone. Katya hoped they would come back when spring returned and the water was warmer.

One morning early, Miyacha came shyly to the door of Katya's house. "Will you come with me?" she said to Katya, and Katya followed without a single question. She and Miyacha walked across the field, past the vegetable garden where Tatuin Marie was digging up the last of the potatoes.

Katya knew that Miyacha thought the garden was silly. She had looked at it carefully one day and told Katya, "We do not have these things called gardens. We gather nuts and greens and berries—all the things we need. The world takes care of us because we are gentle with it."

Katya's old pony was standing in the fog beside the garden. Miyacha pointed to him, "It is a long way, but we will take the pony."

Miyacha walked to the pony and in one quick leap was on his back. The pony's head jerked up in surprise, but he stood still. "Come, get on," said Miyacha.

"But we have no saddle," Katya said.

"Reins, yes. Saddle, no," Miyacha said, so Katya got the leather strap that she used for a leadline and looped it around the pony's nose and pulled him over to the fence. Then she stood on the fence rail and climbed onto the pony. She sat behind Miyacha and kicked her heels into the pony's soft sides.

He walked, and she could feel the muscles moving in his back. They went up and away from the shore. Miyacha held the reins and steered the pony through the tall redwood trees and the ferns growing under them. As they moved along, the sound of the sea followed them.

Up and up they went, past rocks and trees and away from the sea. Ahead of them, Katya could hear the sound of a stream. They followed the stream until it led them out into a high meadow. There, Katya counted at least twenty tall triangular huts made of redwood bark. Women and dogs and children moved among the huts, and smoke rose from the communal cooking fires. Miyacha turned halfway around on the pony and said, "My home."

This time, it was Katya who felt shy. They rode the pony into the circle of huts and slid down from his back. Miyacha tied his reins to a sapling. "So he does not go home without you," she explained.

Katya could not even answer because she was so busy staring around her. The women by the fire were barefoot and wore long skirts that covered them only from waist to ankle. The children ran naked. "There are so many people," Katya whispered to her friend.

"Yes, many people. They are my grand-mothers and my aunts and nieces and neph-ews and uncles. And my father and my mother. And over there my little sisters and brothers. I will not tell you all their names because I know you will not remember them."

She led Katya to one of the larger redwood houses. Outside it, an old woman was weav-ing a basket. The basket was almost complete. Katya could see its shape and the tightly woven pattern of the grasses the old woman used. Beside her on the ground, the woman had piled sedge roots, bulrush roots, and willow and redbud branches. She also had three small baskets containing feathers and white shells and bits of carved abalone shell with its silvery surface.

"Grandmother makes the strongest and most beautiful baskets," Miyacha said. "She weaves in feathers and shells to tell her stories, and the baskets speak to us."

The woman looked up from her basket. Her dark eyes moved slowly over every inch of Katya's body, stopping at her hair. Embarrassed, Katya tried to push her curls back

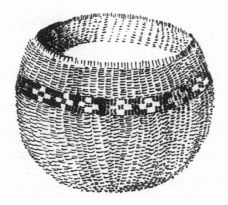

from her face, but the old woman shook her head "no" and reached toward Katya.

"Don't be afraid," Miyacha said. "She only wants to touch your hair."

Katya stepped forward so the woman could run her gnarled fingers across the red curls. The woman spoke to Miyacha in words Katya could not understand.

"She says you are like a beautiful red-winged bird," Miyacha translated. "But come now, because my mother will teach you how she makes the acorn soup."

Miyacha's mother was sitting on the ground near the fire. She was grinding acorn meal with a stone pestle. Like Miyacha's grandmother, she looked carefully at Katya's hair. Katya was afraid everyone in the village would want to touch her hair. For a moment, she wished she had not come.

Then Miyacha spoke to her mother. Her mother replied. Miyacha turned to Katya. "My mother will show you how she makes

44

the soup, and I will explain what she does. When she is finished, you must take the soup home to your Tatuin Marie."

"To Tatuin Marie?" Katya asked. "Does Tatuin Marie like acorn soup?"

"We do not know what Tatuin Marie likes or does not like. We know only that she needs to eat my mother's acorn soup. It will keep her strong and well. Now watch, please. Pay attention, because acorn soup is not easy to make. You can't just gather acorns and throw them into a pot."

Katya nodded and watched Miyacha's mother grind the last of the acorns into flour. Miyacha continued her lesson. "First, you must gather the acorns at the right time of year, when they are still fresh and before the deer or bugs eat them. Then you must dry, crack, and skin them and pound them as my mother does. Then you run water through the flour to get the bitterness out." Miyacha pointed to a basket of wet flour. "Here you see

45

that my mother has already washed the flour for Tatuin Marie's soup."

The wet flour did not look good to Katya, but again she nodded her head. Now Miyacha's mother stood up. She walked away from the fire and returned with a big basket. Katya was surprised to see that the basket was half full of water. How could a basket hold water, she wondered, but she did not dare to ask.

Miyacha's mother set the basket of water on the ground near the fire. Into it she poured the wet flour. She and Miyacha stepped over to the fire and used two sticks each to lift hot rocks out of the fire pit. With the sticks, they carried the rocks to the basket of water and acorn flour. When they dropped the hot stones into the basket, Katya heard the water spit and sizzle. Miyacha's mother added another hot rock, and then stirred the liquid with a long wooden paddle.

"The rocks will make the water boil,"

46

Miyacha said. "Then we will have wonderful acorn soup."

When it was time, Miyacha's mother dipped a small basket into the hot soup and handed it to Katya. Then she filled another for Miyacha and one for herself.

She spoke, and again Miyacha translated to Katya. "My mother says we must eat. Eat, she tells us, and be strong and rejoice in life."

When it was time to go home, Katya was afraid she could not find the way through the tall trees. But Miyacha took the reins of the pony and let them lie loosely on his neck. "Let him go as he wants. He knows the way," she said.

And so Katya returned to Fort Ross with her wise old pony and a basketful of acorn soup for Tatuin Marie.

Chapter 5
And Rejoice

Because Miyacha's village was some miles from Fort Ross and because the pony stopped sometimes to have a bite of grass, the sun went down before Katya was out of the redwood forest. In the dusk, she imagined wild creatures watching from the tree branches, ready to leap onto the pony's back.

Four black-tailed deer ran across the path, and in her fright Katya nearly spilled the basket of soup. An owl hooted somewhere behind her, eerie and sad. Then she began to hear the ocean again. She knew she would be home soon. The pony knew too, and quickened his steps.

By the time Katya reached her house, Papa Petr and Tatuin Marie were waiting and worrying. "Ekaterina, it is dark already! Where have you been?" her father asked sternly.

"We searched for you at the shore and in the orchard," said Tatuin Marie.

"Then we saw that you had taken the pony. We hoped that he, at least, would have sense enough to come home before dark," added Papa Petr.

"I am sorry, Papa Petr. I am sorry, Tatuin Marie. I have been at Miyacha's in the hills, and I have brought a basket of acorn soup for Tatuin Marie." She held out the basket of soup. "Miyacha and her mother say you must eat this soup. They want you to eat and rejoice."

Tatuin Marie put her right hand over her mouth and looked at Papa Petr. "Did they tell

you why I must eat the soup?" she asked
Katya.

"They told me you would know."

Now Tatuin Marie turned to Papa Petr. "I
think that Katya's friend knows our secret,"
she said to him.

"A secret? What secret?" Katya demanded.

"Never mind. But I will eat the soup because I know that it is good for me."

"And we will all rejoice," added Papa Petr,
putting his arm around Tatuin Marie's
shoulders.

But the next day Papa Petr had bad news. The
order had come from Russia. They were to
abandon Fort Ross. "We can stay until everything is sold," he said. "Then we must go."

"Where will we go?" Tatuin Marie was
angry.

"I don't know. Back to Sitka, I suppose.
That is where the boat will take us."

"What about the garden? And the orchard?

And Katya's friend Miyacha? Are we to leave them behind?"

"Papa Petr, I do not want to go! This is our home. You and me and Tatuin Marie."

Her father looked at her sadly. "I know, Katya, but I must think for a few days until I know what will be best. Perhaps there is a way...."

Katya felt like crying. She went outside and found her pony and put her arms around his soft neck. She could ride him away into the woods, she thought. She could go to Miyacha's camp and wait until the Russian ships had sailed away. But if she did that, would she ever see Papa Petr and Tatuin Marie again?

She walked slowly down to shore and along the high cliff until she reached the place of the sea otters. There were no sea otters, but Katya sat and stared at the waves.

From out of nowhere, Miyacha appeared and sat beside her. Miyacha had a basket with her. Katya could not see what was inside because a layer of leaves covered whatever was in there. Perhaps more acorn soup?

Miyacha put the basket on the ground beside her. Then she said, "Don't be sad, Katya. I think that your father and Tatuin Marie will decide to stay. I think they will want your little sister to be born here in California."

"My little sister?"

"Or your little brother. I cannot tell which it will be."

"What do you mean, Miyacha? I have no little sister and no little brother."

"No, but you will have one soon—by the time the otters return, you will have a little brother or sister. Tatuin Marie will have her baby in the spring."

At first, Katya could find no words. Then she said, "Miyacha, how do you know these things? I have not told you we must leave Fort Ross. And even I have not been told about a baby."

"Tatuin Marie once said you do not see what is in front of you. I think that she is right. When you go home today, look at Tatuin Marie. Ask yourself, does she seem different from how she was when the first blossoms came in the orchard?"

"I must go home," Katya said, suddenly eager to see Tatuin Marie. "Will you come with me?"

"Yes, but first you must look in the basket that I have beside me."

"Is it another secret? I am beginning not to like so many secrets."

"This is one you will like." Miyacha lifted the basket and set it on Katya's lap.

The basket weighed almost nothing. Katya could not imagine what was in it, but she pushed back the covering of leaves. And then she saw what Miyacha had made for her. In the basket was a doll. Its head was a bulb of kelp, and its hair was the yarn from a soft red blanket.

"Oh, Miyacha, you have made the seaweed into something beautiful."

"It is the doll I promised. It is *Katya*. See, I have dressed her all in feathers and put pretty stones for her eyes and hair the color of yours."

Katya hugged her doll, and then she hugged her friend. She could feel tears starting in her eyes.

"This is no time for crying," Miyacha said. "Let us go and find your father and Tatuin Marie so they can tell us that you and they—and the baby, when it comes—will stay in California. Then we will rejoice together."

And they did.

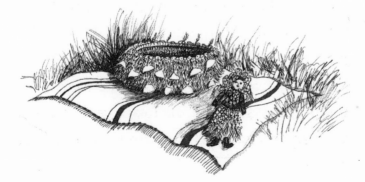

A Little History

At the beginning of the nineteenth century, the California coast was wild, unexplored, and rich with seal and sea otter. Russian explorers had already claimed Russian America (now Alaska) for their country and founded a settlement on Kodiak Island. Then, in 1808, they established New Archangel (later called Sitka) as the permanent headquarters for Russian America. From New Archangel, the Russians hunted for seal and sea otter and began exploring the California coast. All Russian exploration, trade, and settlement in

North America was controlled by a trading company called the Russian-American Company.

As seal and sea otter become more and more scarce, Russians ventured farther south along the California coast. In 1812, the Russian-American Company established Fort Ross as their southernmost outpost. Fort Ross brought the Russians and their Aleut hunters closer to the sea otters. In addition, Fort Ross was expected to grow food for the Russian settlements further north. Russians hoped that Fort Ross would become the "bread basket" for all of Russian America.

In March 1812, Ivan Alexandrovich Kuskov came to Fort Ross with twenty-five Russians and eighty Aleuts (native Alaskans). For hunting, they brought *baidarkas*, swift and maneuverable skin kayaks. The Aleuts made these boats from driftwood and the skins of sea lions. The boats were fast and could go anywhere in search of fur-bearing sea animals, and the Aleuts were very good hunters.

The Russians and the Aleuts who worked for them began building Fort Ross immediately. They completed the stockade in the summer of 1812. The stockade had many cannon, a barracks for Russian employees, two blockhouses, and high, gated walls, but it was more a commercial center than a fort. Several hundred people lived there, and all of them worked for the Russian-American Company.

Many Russians, especially those with families, built their homes outside of the stockade. Most of the Russians at Fort Ross were officers of the Russian-American Company or skilled craftsmen like Katya's father who made everything the settlement needed—from nails to furniture.

The Aleut hunters also lived outside the stockade walls. They built their traditional, partly-underground homes close to the shore where they kept their boats.

East of the stockade were the dwellings of Kashaya Pomo Indians. The Kashaya had been in California for at least 10,000 years before Russians or other explorers arrived. Long before the Russians established their settlement, the Kashaya had a permanent village, May-tee-nee, at Fort Ross. In addition to ancestral villages like May-tee-nee, the Kashaya had temporary camps in different areas along the coast. Where they lived depended on the season. In winter, they lived away from the shore; in summer, they came to the sea to fish and hunt. The Kashaya were a peace-loving people who lived in harmony with the natural world. Their lives were changed drastically by the Russians and the many other people who began flooding into California during the 1800s.

Other structures around the Fort Ross stockade included a windmill, a cattle yard, a threshing floor, farm buildings, bath houses and saunas, a shipyard, a forge, a tannery, and a boathouse. The Russians of Fort Ross made, grew, traded, or caught everything they needed for life in California. They even sold ice from Alaska to the people in San Francisco!

Sea otter skins were very valuable, and many, many otters were killed by the hunters. By 1820, there were only a few sea otters left, so the people of Fort Ross had to concentrate on agriculture and raising farm animals. These efforts were not very successful. It was difficult to grow crops because of coastal fog, gophers, mice, and blackbirds, and the settlers at Fort Ross were interested in hunting and trading, not farming.

Several farms were established in more sheltered areas away from the coast, and these were successful. The Russians also experimented with fruit trees, including peaches, quince, apples, grapes, cherries, and pears. Some of the trees planted by the Russians at Fort Ross still bear fruit today. The

Russians also raised several thousand head of cattle, horses, mules, sheep, and other animals. Agriculture peaked in the early 1830s, but Fort Ross was never as productive as the Russian-American Company hoped.

Finally, in 1839, the Russian government decided that Fort Ross was too far away from the rest of Russia, too difficult to manage, and not profitable enough. Fort Ross was offered for sale, along with all its buildings, equipment, and livestock. In 1841, John Sutter purchased Fort Ross for $30,000.

Most of the Russian and native Alaskan inhabitants of Fort Ross left on ships bound for Sitka. Others, like Katya and her family, stayed and made California their home.